STAR WARS®
REVENGE OF THE SITH™
Trivia Quest

LUCAS BOOKS

Random House
New York

www.randomhouse.com/kids
www.starwars.com

ISBN: 0-375-82613-0

MANUFACTURED IN CANADA
First Edition 10 9 8 7 6 5 4 3 2 1

WAR! The galaxy is in turmoil. The Jedi and the clone army are desperately trying to defend the Republic against Count Dooku and the Confederacy of Independent Systems. Although the dark side clouds everything, the Jedi must struggle to maintain control, or the Republic will crumble.

You can help the Republic battle the evil Count Dooku, his Confederacy of Independent Systems, and the Sith Lords, who are secretly behind the evil throughout the galaxy.

Your quest awaits you in the form of questions. With each successful completion of one of the four levels, you will have helped the Republic and the Jedi in their fight against evil. Be careful! These questions become more difficult as you progress, as do the missions you face. Once you have completed your tasks in the first four levels, you will be taken into the future to face a special secret level! Take your time, as the fate of the galaxy may be in your hands. As Master Qui-Gon Jinn once said, "Feel—don't think. Use your instincts."

The Jedi, the Republic, and the citizens of the galaxy are counting on you—you may be their only hope!

LEVEL ONE

Help Obi-Wan Rescue Chancellor Palpatine!

10 Questions (10 points)

Hello, young Jedi! It's Obi-Wan Kenobi. The Jedi Council has sent Anakin Skywalker and me out on a very important mission—one that could determine the future of the Republic. We need your help!

It seems we have a massive problem. Separatist agents have kidnapped Chancellor Palpatine! Anakin and I are on our way to rescue him. We'll need all the help we can get. There are droid fighters everywhere, and who knows what new tricks the Separatists have up their sleeves.

Are you up for it? If so, you'll need to use your Jedi training. Take your time answering the following questions and you might help Anakin and me rescue the Chancellor.

If you fail to help us with this mission, I'm sure the Council can come up with an appropriate task to get you back on track with your Jedi training. Maybe they'll choose to send you to the Rolling Shaak Corral on Naboo. The wranglers always need help cleaning out the shaaks' pens, and all that raking will give you plenty of time to reflect on your failure.

May the Force be with you, young one, and with all of us!

I. Character Knowledge

1. The Chancellor of the Galactic Senate is:
   a. Valorum   b. Pontoon   c. Palpatine   d. Goitrous

2. Anakin Skywalker and Obi-Wan Kenobi are _ _ _ _.

3. The Sith Lord in charge of the Separatists is:
   a. General Grievous   b. Darth Vader
   c. Darth Maul   d. Count Dooku

4. The Grand Army of the Republic is made up of:
   a. Volunteers   b. Clones   c. Wookiees   d. Slaves

5. The droid general aboard the Separatist cruiser is known as:
   a. General Mills   b. General Bilious
   c. General Grievous   d. General Plagueis

II. Mission Knowledge

6. **True or False:** Chancellor Palpatine thinks that Obi-Wan and Anakin will be able to defeat Count Dooku by themselves.

7. Who does Anakin sense aboard the Separatist cruiser?
   a. Count Dooku   b. General Grievous
   c. Plo Koon   d. Yaddle

8. **True or False:** Anakin defeats Count Dooku.

9. **True or False:** When Anakin and Obi-Wan rescue Chancellor Palpatine, he is all alone.

10. **True or False:** Anakin, R2-D2, Obi-Wan Kenobi, and Chancellor Palpatine use Anakin's Jedi starfighter to escape the Separatist cruiser.

Discover how helpful you were to the Republic and the Jedi by turning to page 60 and checking your answers. Score 1 point for every correct answer.

Write your score here _____

A perfect score is 10 points.

If you scored 6 points or less, you must face Master Yoda. But before you do, you have one last chance to prove yourself—the Coruscant Skyline Bonus Question. Answer it correctly and Master Yoda just might spare you the special trip he's got in mind!

If you scored 7 points or more, try the Coruscant Skyline Bonus Question anyway. Your Jedi skills are honed enough that I'm sure you'll do a fine job.

 CORUSCANT SKYLINE BONUS QUESTION

The clone leader of Squad Seven is:
a. Odd Ball
b. Red Leader
c. Red Seven
d. Odd Square

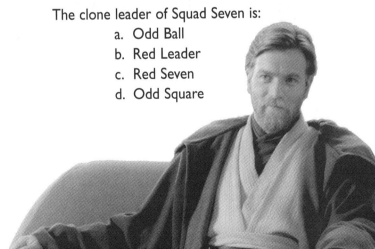

a. Odd Ball

Were you correct? If so, turn to page 11 to continue your journey.

If you were incorrect, and you scored 6 points or less on the Level I quiz, then you must face Master Yoda. Read below to see what he has in store for you.

Scored, you have, 6 points or less. . . .

Failed, you have, to assist your fellow Jedi in their mission to rescue the Chancellor. Succeeded, they have, in rescuing him—thanks not to you!

Although successful you were not in aiding Master Obi-Wan and his Padawan, strong are you in the Force. Much training, you still need. A special mission will allow you to meditate on the Force.

To the Rolling Shaak Corral on Naboo, will you go. Report to Phildro Exxu, owner of the corral. Assist the wranglers at this ranch, you will, cleaning the shaak pens and tending to various duties. Despair not! Your tasks there, powerful will they make you. Strong! Return, you will, more mindful and more attuned to the Force. Spend your hours in the pens concentrating on the Force, and your next mission with the Jedi, successful will it be.

Pack your bags, you will—you leave in the morning. Go!

LEVEL TWO

Help Obi-Wan Defeat General Grievous!

50 Questions (50 points)

Greetings again, young Padawan! This mission is one of the most important in the history of the Jedi Order. The Jedi Council has learned that the dreaded General Grievous and his troops are on the planet Utapau. The Separatists are weak. Anakin Skywalker defeated Count Dooku, their leader. Now we can swoop in and rid the galaxy of their evil influence once and for all. With General Grievous out of the way, we hope that Chancellor Palpatine will give up his emergency powers and reinstate the great democracy that has ruled the galaxy for the past thousand years.

Utapau is a mysterious planet filled with sinkholes that can contain strange and dangerous creatures such as nos monsters. Finding Grievous will not be easy. We've got two clone brigades accompanying us, but that might not be enough! General Grievous is brilliant and treacherous. To make matters worse, he has been trained in lightsaber combat. He collects the lightsabers of Jedi he's defeated, but I don't intend to let him get mine!

Be mindful, and concentrate on your feelings. Don't give in to anger or hate—those emotions lead to the dark side. Let the Force flow through you on this mission and you will do fine. To your ship!

I. CHARACTER KNOWLEDGE

Identify the following characters:

1. _ _ _ _ _ _ _ _ _   _ _ _ _ _ _ _ _

2. _ _ _ _ _ _ _

_ _ _ _ _ _ _ _ _ _

3. _ _ _ - _ _ _ _ _ _ _ _ _ _

4. _ _ _ _ _ _   _ _ _ _ _

5. _ _ _ _ _ _ _ _ _ _

_ _ _ _ _ _ _ _ _ _

6. According to Obi-Wan Kenobi, the first Jedi rule is:
   a. Maintain clean inner ears
   b. Survive
   c. Practice your lightsaber techniques
   d. Meditate

7. **True or False:** According to Obi-Wan, Sith Lords are his specialty.

8. Who says the following: "Never an elevator when you need one."
   a. Anakin Skywalker   b. R2-D2
   c. Mon Mothma   d. Obi-Wan Kenobi

9. General Grievous collects:
   a. Astrocomics   b. Spare droid parts
   c. Lightsabers   d. Electrostaffs

10. Anakin is married to _ _ _ _ _ _ _ _ _ _ _ _.

11. Mace Windu is a member of:
    a. The Senate   b. The Jedi Council
    c. The Republic Galactic Guard   d. The Sith

12. **True or False:** Anakin has a nightmare involving Padmé.

13. **True or False:** Anakin considers Chancellor Palpatine to be a friend.

Identify the following characters:

 14. _ _ _ _ _ _ _ _ _

15. _ _ _ _ _

_ _ _ _ _ _ _

 16. _ _ _ _

_ _ _ _ _ _

17. _ _ _ _

18. _ _ _ _ _ _ _

_ _ _ _ _

19. _ _ _ _ _ _ _ _ _

20. _ _ - _ _ _ -

_ _ _ _ _

14

II. DROIDS AND VEHICLES

21. Obi-Wan's droid aboard his red Jedi starfighter is:

    a. R5-D4   b. R3-G9   c. R4-P17   d. R2-D2

22. **True or False:** R2-D2 has rockets in his legs that allow him to fly.

23. Obi-Wan's starfighter is attacked by:

    a. Protocol droids   b. Buzz droids

    c. Battle droids   d. Droidekas

24. Buzz droids are deployed from:

    a. Missiles   b. Astromech droids

    c. Slingshots   d. Cannons

25. Buzz droids are equipped with:

    a. Lightsabers   b. Night vision

    c. Plasma torches   d. Hydraulic lifts

26. R2-D2 is:

    a. A protocol droid   b. An astromech droid

    c. A Gonk droid   d. A pit droid

27. **True or False:** According to Anakin, battle droids are worthy opponents and one should be cautious around them.

Identify the following:

28. _ _ _ _ _ _ _ _ _ _ _ _ _

29. _ _ _ _ _ _ _ _ _ _

30. _

31. _ _ _ _ _ _ _ _ _ _ _ _ _

32. _ _ _ _ _

_ _ _ _ _ _ _ _ _ _ _ _ _

33. _

34. _

35. _ _ _ _ _ _ _ _ _ -

_ _ _ _ _ _

III. Aliens and Planets

36. Obi-Wan and Anakin rescue Chancellor Palpatine in a ship orbiting the planet:
    a. Tatooine   b. Coruscant   c. Aduba-3   d. Corellia

37. Anakin's home planet is:
    a. Tatooine   b. Dantooine   c. Dagobah   d. Alderaan

38. Nute Gunray is a:
    a. Rodian   b. Mon Calamari
    c. Neimoidian   d. Twi'lek

39. Representative Jar Jar Binks is a:
    a. Human   b. Sullustan   c. Jawa   d. Gungan

40. Bail Organa is from the planet _ _ _ _ _ _ _ _.

IV. Galactic Politics

41. **True or False:** When Count Dooku is defeated, Mace Windu states that the time has come for peace.

42. According to Anakin, if the Chancellor hadn't been kidnapped, he and Obi-Wan would still be fighting in:
    a. Geonosis
    b. The Perlemian Trade Route Wars
    c. The Outer Rim Sieges
    d. The Rishi Maze Conundrum

43. **True or False:** Darth Sidious expresses regret over Darth Tyranus's death.

44. **True or False:** Mace Windu believes that the Clone Wars should continue after General Grievous is defeated.

45. **True or False:** Chancellor Palpatine confesses to Anakin that he is a Sith Lord.

46. **True or False:** Chancellor Palpatine takes control of the Jedi Council away from the Senate and makes the Council report directly to him.

47. As Chancellor Palpatine's first action in his direct control over the Jedi Council, he:
    a. Makes them stop wearing those cumbersome robes
    b. Demands that they gather more troops to aid the Republic
    c. Sends Yoda to Kashyyyk
    d. Makes Anakin Skywalker his personal representative on the Jedi Council

48. **True or False:** Obi-Wan and the Jedi Council ask Anakin to spy on Chancellor Palpatine.

49. Mon Mothma hopes to form an alliance in the Senate to:
    a. Make sure that the Senate building gets redecorated before the Galactic Fair
    b. Preserve democracy in the Republic
    c. Stop polluting the rivers of Naboo
    d. Assist Chancellor Palpatine in his campaign against the Separatists

50. **True or False:** A group of Senators organizes an alliance to oppose Chancellor Palpatine.

The battle on Utapau was a tough one, but General Grievous has fallen. However, darker things are happening in the galaxy. It's my guess that Chancellor Palpatine hasn't called for an end to the war. We must regroup with the other Jedi to plan our actions—it appears that the clones have turned against us! Your part in the upcoming battle will be decided by how well you did on Utapau.

Turn to page 61 and check your answers. Score 1 point for every correct answer.

Write your score here _____

A perfect score is 50 points.

If you scored 34 points or less, you have one last chance to redeem yourself—the Sizzling Sinkhole Bonus Question. If you answer that correctly, the Jedi might, in these desperate times, overlook your failings.

If you scored 35 points or more, turn to page 23 to continue your journey. You might want to try the Sizzling Sinkhole Bonus Question anyway, just to make yourself feel better after that long, hard battle!

SIZZLING SINKHOLE BONUS QUESTION

The administrator on Utapau who warns Obi-Wan that General Grievous and thousands of battle droids are hidden on the planet is:

    a. Tia Leone   b. Tion Medon
    c. Tito Puente   d. Tina Yothers

SIZZLING SINKHOLE BONUS QUESTION ANSWER

b. Tion Medon

Were you correct? If you were, turn to page 23 to go on your next mission.

If you were incorrect, and scored 34 points or less on the Level II quiz, then I should have left you back there with that nos monster we ran into! But that's against the Jedi Code.

I've gotten word that the clones are revolting against Jedi across the galaxy, so I really don't have time to think up an appropriate punishment. I have to get back to Coruscant to try to figure out what's going on and rescue any Jedi in trouble.

You need to stay here. The Utapauns are friendly beings, and they're going to need your assistance collecting all the broken droids that are littering their streets.

What's that? You didn't leave your family to become a garbage collector? Well, you should have thought about that when you were busy fidgeting around with hologames instead of studying. When this is all over, I'll come back to get you and we can start your training anew. For now, you're safer here, believe me.

May the Force be with you.

Help Yoda Escape the Clones on Kashyyyk!

60 Questions (60 points)

Very important to the Republic, the planet of Kashyyyk is! When overrun it became by droid armies, vowed, did I, to rescue Kashyyyk from the clutches of evil. Friendly, am I, with the Wookiees.

Now happened, something has, that is dark and mysterious—turning on their allies, the clones are! Sense, I do, the dark side at work. Back to Coruscant, I must go. Bring Palpatine to justice, we must, if we are to end this war!

An escape pod nearby, Chewbacca and Tarfful told me there is. Get to it, we must! Come—fight our way, we will, through the clone army in the jungles of Kashyyyk. Powerful allies, Wookiees are. But by the clones outnumbered, we are. The Force to guide us, we will need!

Answer the following questions and complete your mission. Succeed, you must!

I. CONFEDERACY OF INDEPENDENT SYSTEMS KNOWLEDGE

1. General Grievous has asked the leaders of the Confederacy of Independent Systems to retreat to the planet:
   a. Alderaan
   b. Ord Mantell
   c. Mustafar
   d. Tatooine

2. Nute Gunray is Viceroy of the:
   a. InterGalactic Banking Clan
   b. Trade Federation
   c. Geonosian Droid Foundries
   d. Galactic Republic

3. The Settlement Officer for the Trade Federation is:
   a. Ponda Baba
   b. Lott Dod
   c. Daultay Dofine
   d. Rune Haako

4. The Magistrate for the Corporate Alliance is:
   a. Passel Argente
   b. Ree Blankuna
   c. Don Na'Tella
   d. Plu Neeku

5. The Chairman of the InterGalactic Banking Clan is:
   a. Son Hull
   b. San Hill
   c. Cen Holl
   d. Sen Hall

6. **True or False:** Nute Gunray believes General Grievous when Grievous tells him the Separatists will be safe in their new, secret location.

7. Who talks to General Grievous via hologram while Grievous is on Utapau?
   a. Count Dooku
   b. Darth Tyranus
   c. Darth Maul
   d. Darth Sidious

8. **True or False:** General Grievous is worried that Obi-Wan will be able to defeat him on Utapau.

9. According to the super battle droid who meets General Grievous as he's landing on Utapau, the planet is:
   a. Ready for deforestation   b. Devoid of life
   c. Secure   d. Lacking supplies

10. Po Nudo is a:
    a. Member of the Trade Federation
    b. Senator
    c. Shi'ido Changeling
    d. Jedi Knight in disguise

II. CHARACTER IDENTIFICATION

Identify the following characters:

11. _ _ _ _ _ _ _ _ _ _

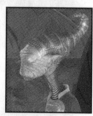

12. _ _ _ _ _ _

13. _ _ _ _ _ _ _ _ _ _ _ _ _

14. _ _ _ _ _ _ _ _ _ _ _ _

15. _ _ _ _ _ _ _ _

III. Weapons Identification

Identify the following weapons:

16. _ _ _ _ _ _ _ _ _ _ _ _ _

17. _ _ _ _ _ _ _ _ _ _ _ _ _ _

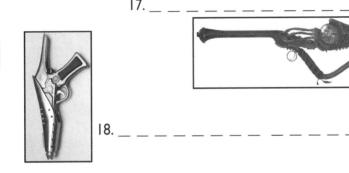

18. _ _ _ _ _ _ _ _ _ _ _ _ _ _ _ _

19. _ _ _ _ _ _ _ _ _ _ _ _ _ _ _

20. _ _ _ _ _ _ _ _ _ _ _ _ _ _ _ _ _

21. _ _ _ _ _ _ _ _ _ _ _ _ _ ,_

_ _ _ _ _ _ _ _ _ _

Using this list, identify the following parts of Obi-Wan's lightsaber.

a. Activator b. Power-cell housing c. Blade emitter d. Handgrip

22. __

23. __

24. __

25. __

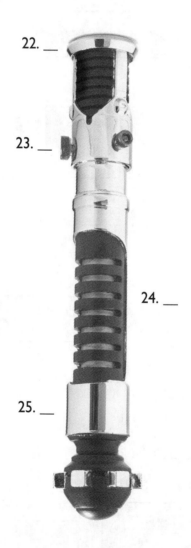

IV. Droids and Vehicles

Identify the following droids:

26. _ _ _ _ _ _ _ _ _ _ _

27. _ _ _ _ _ _ _ _

     _ _ _ _ _

28. _ - _ _ _

29. _ _ _ _ _ _ _ _ _ _ _

30. _ _ _ _ _ _ _ _ _ _

     _ _ _ _ _

31. C-3PO is a:
    a. Battle droid
    b. Astromech droid
    c. Protocol droid
    d. Super battle droid

32. ARC-170 starfighters were created and put into use in the Republic army immediately following the battle of:
    a. Taanab
    b. Cato Neimoidia
    c. Sullust
    d. Gundark Alley

33. **True or False:** General Grievous's wheel bike can walk and fly.

34. AT-RT stands for:
    a. All Terrain Roller Transport
    b. Astro Tech Recon Tank
    c. Alternate Travel Recon Tank
    d. All Terrain Recon Transport

35. **True or False:** V-wing fighters do not require a hyperdrive ring to jump into lightspeed.

V. Aliens and Creatures

Identify the following:

36. _ _ _ _ _ _

37. _ _ _   _ _ _ _ _ _ _

38. _ _ _ - _ _ _ _

39. _ _ _ _ _ _ _ _

40. _ _ _ _ _

41. **True or False:** Padmé is pregnant when Anakin turns to the dark side.

42. **True or False:** Yoda thinks it's a great idea for Chancellor Palpatine to take direct control of the Jedi Council.

43. **True or False:** Anakin is upset with the news that he's been appointed to the Jedi Council.

44. After the Republic defeats the Separatists on the planet Saleucami, Jedi Master Vos takes his troops to the planet:
    a. Boz Pity   b. Godstar 23   c. Aduba-3   d. Chronelle

45. **True or False:** The Jedi Council accepts Anakin with no hesitation.

46. What does the Chancellor do to oversee all of the star systems in the Republic?
    a. Forces all beings to get v-chips implanted in their brains
    b. Appoints governors
    c. Brainwashes everyone
    d. Compels every being above the age of twenty-one to enlist in the Republic army

47. **True or False:** Chancellor Palpatine was Senator Amidala's Ambassador when she was Queen of Naboo.

48. Kashyyyk is very important to the Republic because:
    a. It is the largest galactic supplier of mekon berries
    b. Wookiee pelts make really comfortable jackets
    c. It's the main navigation route for the southwestern quadrant
    d. Wookiees are known for their down-home hospitality

49. **True or False:** Anakin is the youngest Jedi ever to be appointed to the Jedi Council.

50. **True or False:** Yoda thinks the prophecy stating that Anakin Skywalker is the Chosen One to bring balance to the Force may have been misread.

51. What makes Padmé think her baby is going to be a boy?
    a. Her motherly intuition
    b. A visit to the medical droid
    c. Her psychic advisor told her so
    d. All first-born children in her family have been boys

52. Padmé begs Anakin to ask the Chancellor to:
    a. Continue attacking the Separatists until they are destroyed
    b. Send the Separatists out of the galaxy when they are defeated
    c. Stop the fighting and let diplomacy resume
    d. Heighten security around the Senate

53. Who does Anakin sense has been visiting Padmé's apartment?
    a. Jar Jar Binks
    b. Chancellor Palpatine
    c. Obi-Wan Kenobi
    d. Ex-Chancellor Valorum

54. Who says the following: "Wookiee good . . . eat Wookiee!"
    a. Tarfful   b. Yoda
    c. Clone Commander Gree   d. Awdree'sta Peena

55. **True or False:** Tarfful does not survive the clone attack on Kashyyyk.

56. **True or False:** Yoda really likes the mud bath he's gotten on Kashyyyk.

57. How does Chewbacca access the escape pod Yoda uses to blast off from Kashyyyk?
    a. He goes to the nearest hangar
    b. He pulls a tree limb to reveal the pod
    c. He rips some shrubs off a hole in the ground
    d. He sends a signal to some soldiers who prepare the craft for Yoda

58. **True or False:** The seeker drones chasing Obi-Wan Kenobi on Utapau are successful in capturing him.

59. What rumor did C-3PO tell R2-D2 about in Padmé's apartment on Coruscant?
    a. That all droids are going to be forced into mandatory tune-ups once a month
    b. That droids are going to be banished
    c. That all protocol droids are going to have their memories wiped
    d. That all droids are going to be trained for battle

60. What order does Darth Sidious ask the clone commanders to execute?
    a. Order Sixty-five
    b. Order Sixty-three
    c. Order Sixty-seven
    d. Order Sixty-six

Blasted off, have we, from the planet Kashyyyk, and avoided the attack of the clones successfully. Chewbacca and Tarfful, helpful were they, indeed! But how helpful were you in our mission?

Turn, you will, to page 62 and find out. For every correct answer, score 1 point.

Write your score here _____

A perfect score is 60 points.

If scored, you did, 39 points or less, one last chance, have you, to prove your Jedi abilities. Try the Kashyyyk Crusher Question. If answer correctly this question, you do, then you have not failed the Jedi Order.

If scored, you did, 40 points or more, turn to page 39 to continue your quest. Try the Kashyyyk Crusher Question anyway to hone your Jedi abilities!

KASHYYYK CRUSHER QUESTION

What is the name of the language that Wookiees speak?

    a. Shyriiwook   b. Shuriiwooke
    c. Shalliwook   d. Shorrellewook

KASHYYYK CRUSHER
QUESTION ANSWER

a. Shyriiwook

Get it right, did you? If so, turn to page 39 to continue your journey.

If get it wrong, you did, and 39 points or less, you scored, on the Level III quiz, help on Kashyyyk, you did not. You disappoint me, young Padawan. Tried, we did, to train you well, but to our lessons, you did not listen. Now return, I must, to Coruscant. Chewie and Tarfful, an escape pod have supplied me.

Asked me, the Wookiees have, if stay here on Kashyyyk, you could, to help them clean the battle debris from their swamps and lakes. Very conscious of their surroundings, the Wookiees are—revere nature, they do. Stay here with them and assist them in tending to their natural resources and redeem yourself, you will. The balance of life on this planet will thank you, as will the Wookiees.

The Wookiee language—difficult it is to master, but learn it, you must. Patience and courage will make your stay on Kashyyyk a good experience. Not strong enough, are you, to face what lies in the galaxy right now—a great favor I am doing you by telling you to stay here! Goodbye, my young friend.

50 Questions (50 points)

Dark times have fallen on the Republic, my young apprentice. The clone army has turned on the Jedi and destroyed all we have protected for the past thousand years.

The Jedi Temple is in ruins. I have discovered that my apprentice Anakin Skywalker has turned to the dark side. He is now helping Darth Sidious hunt down the last of the Jedi. Although it pains my heart, I know what I must do.

I am going to the planet Mustafar to confront Anakin. It is a grim mission, but one that must be done. The prophecy, according to my Master, Qui-Gon Jinn, stated that Anakin would be the one to bring balance to the Force. It appears that prophecy might have been misread!

I can use your help. If even one Jedi life is spared, there may yet be hope for the future of the galaxy. Take your time in answering the following questions—let the Force flow through you. Your feelings will tell you what is correct.

Remember, patience! If we fail this mission, there will be even darker days ahead.

May the Force be with you always.

I. Sith Knowledge

1. **True or False:** According to Mace Windu, the dark side of the Force surrounds Chancellor Palpatine.

2. Chancellor Palpatine is actually:
   a. Darth Plagueis
   b. A Jedi Master
   c. Darth Sidious
   d. A shape-shifting alien in disguise

3. According to Chancellor Palpatine, Obi-Wan Kenobi may not be fit for his assignment to Utapau because:
   a. He's way out of shape
   b. His judgment has been clouded by a "certain Senator"
   c. He's turning to the dark side of the Force
   d. General Grievous is an excellent swordsman

4. **True or False:** The Sith have been operating secretly in the galaxy for a very long time.

5. Chancellor Palpatine tells Anakin that he can teach him to:
   a. Keep people from dying
   b. Be the best pilot in the galaxy
   c. Be an expert with his lightsaber
   d. Bring peace to the galaxy

6. There are usually only two Sith Lords at one time because:
   a. The apprentices are so hungry for power they would keep turning on their Masters
   b. There are too few beings who can construct lightsabers with red blades
   c. All that black clothing would be too obvious
   d. Sith Masters need to live in solitude.

7. To whom does Chancellor Palpatine first reveal that he is a Sith Lord?
   a. Mace Windu
   b. Obi-Wan Kenobi
   c. Yoda
   d. Anakin Skywalker

8. According to Chancellor Palpatine, the dark side of the Force is a pathway to many abilities some conside   e:
   a. Unlawful
   b. Extraterrestrial
   c. Unnatural
   d. Illogical

9. **True or False:** According to Chancellor Palpatine, the Jedi and the Sith are the same in almost every way.

10. What happens to Darth Sidious as he tries to intensify his powers?
    a. His eyes become yellow
    b. His skin catches on fire
    c. He melts
    d. His nose turns red

11. Why does Anakin turn to the dark side of the Force?
    a. He wants to rule the galaxy
    b. He wants the power to shoot Force lightning
    c. He wants to be able to stop death
    d. He likes the outfits

12. When Anakin finally turns to the dark side, he becomes:
    a. Darth Pahl
    b. Darth Vader
    c. Darth Pinatubo
    d. Darth Malicious

13. **True or False:** Darth Vader defeats Obi-Wan Kenobi on Mustafar.

14. According to Darth Sidious, who killed Padmé?
    a. Obi-Wan Kenobi
    b. Darth Sidious
    c. General Grievous
    d. Darth Vader

II. JEDI KNOWLEDGE

Identify these members of the Jedi Council:

15. _ _ _ _ _ _ _ _ _

16. _ _ _ _ _ _ _ _ _ _

17. _ _ _ _ _ _ _

18. In the film *Revenge of the Sith,* how many Jedi do we see for sure survived the attack of the clones and the Sith?

    a. 5   b. 3   c. 4   d. 2

19. What coded retreat signal did the Jedi receive?

    a. That the war is over and all Jedi must return to the Jedi Temple

    b. That the war is over and the Sith have won—all Jedi should hide

    c. That the war is not over and all Jedi should stay alert

    d. That the war is over and there will be a barbecue on Kashyyyk

III. PLANETS

20. On what planet was Ki-Adi-Mundi attacked by his clone troops?

    a. Mygeeto   b. Mylondo   c. Gymeeto   d. Remeato

21. Who responds to the emergency code message Obi-Wan Kenobi sends out after he's attacked by his clone troops?

    a. Master Yoda   b. Chancellor Palpatine

    c. Senator Bail Organa   d. Anakin Skywalker

22. The medical center to which Padmé is taken is on an asteroid at:

    a. Polits Moffa   b. Polis Massa

    c. Puless Nassa   d. Pelless Hassa

23. **True or False:** Obi-Wan Kenobi takes refuge on the planet Dantooine.

24. Yoda retreats to the planet:
    a. Xagobah   b. Bobah
    c. Dagobah   d. Ed'ie-Beal

IV. GALACTIC HAPPENINGS

25. **True or False:** According to Chancellor Palpatine, *he* is the Senate.

26. **True or False:** Chancellor Palpatine uses Mace Windu's lightsaber to fight the Jedi.

27. Why do Mace and the other Jedi appear at Chancellor Palpatine's office?
    a. To congratulate him on the victory against the Separatists
    b. To arrest him
    c. To bring him a blueberry pie
    d. To bring him a petition signed by a majority in the Senate

28. **True or False:** Anakin does not help kill Mace Windu.

29. **True or False:** Jedi Master Adi Gallia is attacked while flying a Jedi fighter.

30. According to the clone troopers guarding the entrance of the Jedi Temple, the building is on fire:
    a. Because of a lightsaber mishap
    b. Because there's been a rebellion
    c. Because faulty wiring caught something on fire
    d. Due to improper storing of flammable fuels

31. Anakin tells Padmé that the Jedi Council has tried to:
    a. Force him to resign
    b. Destroy all of the clones
    c. Overthrow the Republic
    d. Join forces with the Separatists

32. Darth Sidious tells Darth Vader to go to Mustafar to:
    a. Destroy the Separatist Council
    b. Collect some crystals to construct a lightsaber
    c. Battle Obi-Wan Kenobi
    d. Regroup with the Separatist Council to discuss their next actions

33. After the clones attack the Jedi, the Separatists
    a. Send their droid armies to Coruscant
    b. Shut down their droid armies
    c. Attempt to overthrow Chancellor Palpatine
    d. Celebrate their victory

34. **True or False:** The Jedi guarding the decimated Jedi Temple are actually clones.

35. In the Senate, Chancellor Palpatine blames his scars on:
    a. Falling over a railing
    b. An attack on his person by the Jedi
    c. A very bad speeder accident
    d. A fight with the clones

36. **True or False:** Bail Organa thinks that the Senate will go along with what Chancellor Palpatine has been saying about the Jedi.

37. **True or False:** Chancellor Palpatine gives power back to the Senate after the war is over.

The tide has turned. The dark side has won—for now. The young twins are safely hidden away from their father, and the only thing we can do now is wait.

Although we did not win this battle, there are Jedi still alive in the galaxy. There is hope for the future. Turn to page 63, add up your score, and see how you did. Score 1 point for every correct answer.

Write your score here _____

A perfect score is 50 points.

If you scored 34 points or less, you can still say you were helpful in our struggle against the Sith by trying out the Mustafarian Twister Question. If you answer that question correctly, you helped the Jedi considerably.

If you scored 35 points or more, you were already a great help to the Jedi, despite our inability to defeat the dark side of the Force. You can turn to page 53 to see how much you know about the times of the Empire. Try the Mustafarian Twister Question anyway, for old times' sake.

MUSTAFARIAN TWISTER QUESTION

Qui-Gon Jinn is going to teach Yoda how to merge with the Force at will and maintain individual consciousness. Who originally perfected this ability?

    a. Darth Plagueis   b. A Shaman of the Whills
    c. A Dathomir Witch   d. Exar Kun

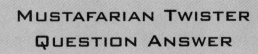
b. A Shaman of the Whills

Were you correct? If so, jump to the future and see if you can fare as well there as you did in the last days of the Republic.

If you were incorrect, and you scored 34 points or less on the Level IV quiz, you must live with the knowledge that our galaxy is now in the hands of the Emperor, and will be for a very long time. Read on for a special message from the Emperor himself!

Greetings, My Young Friend!

I really must congratulate you. With your help, I have finally managed to do what the Sith have been plotting for hundreds of years. The galaxy is now mine.

Darth Vader and I have dismantled the Jedi Council and taken over the Senate. We are now in the process of building the ultimate weapon— the Death Star. With its completion, no one in the galaxy will dare defy us! Since you were such a help in our battle against the Jedi, how would you like to come work for me as one of my personal guards? It's an offer you can't refuse.

The Jedi are destroyed. Long live the Empire!

BONUS LEVEL

Help Restore Balance to the Force

30 Questions (30 points)

Welcome to the cause, my young friend. I am Luke Skywalker, Jedi Knight and member of the Rebellion against the evil Galactic Empire. Our numbers are small, but we are determined. More importantly, we have the Force on our side.

The Rebellion is readying itself for a massive attack against the Empire and we can use your help! Construction has begun on yet another battle station, and our troops are going to attack before it becomes fully operational. We would like you to assist us in defeating this enemy once and for all, and you can do so by answering the following questions.

Take your time. This is an important battle, and with your help we can win it and restore peace to this great galaxy.

I. CHARACTER KNOWLEDGE

1. Who is a member of the Imperial Senate on a diplomatic mission to Alderaan:
   a. Prince Xizor
   b. Princess Leia
   c. Grand Moff Tarkin
   d. Captain Antilles

2. Who do Obi-Wan and Luke Skywalker meet in Mos Eisley:
   a. Tarfful and Greedo
   b. Chewbacca and Wuher
   c. Han Solo and Chewbacca
   d. Aurra Sing and Boba Fett

3. Luke Skywalker receives Jedi training in the swamp from:
   a. Yaddle   b. Yarael Poof
   c. Yoda   d. Yella

Identify the following characters:

4. _ _ _ _ _

   _ _ _ _ _ _ _ _ _

5. _ _ _ _ _ _ _

   _ _ _ _ _ _

6. _ _ _ _ _ _ _ _ _

   _ _ _ _ _

7. _ _ _ _ _   _ _ _ _

II. Planets

8. Luke Skywalker is from the planet _ _ _ _ _ _ _ _.

9. Obi-Wan Kenobi senses a disturbance in the Force when the Death Star destroys:
   a. Dantooine   b. Alderaan   c. Yavin 4   d. Dagobah

10. Cloud City floats above a gas giant planet called:
    a. Bestoon   b. Belbin   c. Bespin   d. Belwoin

11. The Rebel Alliance sets up a base on this icy planet:
    a. Hith   b. Goth   c. Hethe   d. Hoth

12. Luke Skywalker receives the majority of his Jedi training on the planet:
    a. Dagobah   b. Dantooine   c. Muunilinst   d. Xagobah

13. According to Darth Vader, reports have stated that the Rebel Alliance is massing near:
    a. Sullust   b. Bogden   c. Naboo   d. Hoth

14. The final battle between the Empire and the Rebellion takes place on and above the forest moon of:
    a. Endora   b. Endor   c. Fondor   d. Gandor

15. **True or False:** Tatooine has plenty of water.

III. Aliens and Creatures

16. R2-D2 and C-3PO are captured on Tatooine by:
    a. Ugnaughts   b. Jawas
    c. Tusken Raiders   d. Kowakian monkey-lizards

17. Greedo, the bounty hunter who captures Han Solo in Mos Eisley, is a:

    a. Radian   b. Rolian   c. Restian   d. Rodian

18. The Tusken Raiders ride furry creatures called:

    a. Mammoths   b. Banthas

    c. Eopies   d. Falumpasets

19. The Rebels use these creatures to travel short distances while on the planet Hoth:

    a. Tauntauns   b. Trandoshans   c. Troodons   d. Tom-Toms

Identify the following:

20. _ _ _ _ _ _ _ _ _

    _ _ _ _ _

21. _ _ _ _ _ _

22. _ _ _ _

23. _ _ _ _

24. _ _ _ _ _ _ _ _

IV. DROIDS

25. **True or False:** C-3PO is carrying the technical readouts to the Death Star when Luke Skywalker's uncle purchases him on Tatooine.

26. **True or False:** R2-D2 is Uncle Owen's first pick when he's buying astromech droids from the Jawas.

27. **True or False:** R2-D2 is able to locate Princess Leia's cell when Luke is searching for her on the Death Star.

28. **True or False:** R2-D2 survives the Rebellion's assault on the Death Star.

29. After C-3PO is blasted apart in Cloud City, this character puts him back together:
   a. Han Solo   b. Chewbacca   c. Princess Leia   d. R2-D2

30. **True or False:** The Ewoks regard C-3PO as a god.

We've destroyed the second Death Star, along with the Emperor!

Now we're going to have a big celebration. But before you're invited, we've got to find out how well you did in helping us.

Turn to page 64 and check your answers. Score 1 point for every correct answer.

Write your score here _____

A perfect score is 30 points.

If you scored 19 points or less, you can still get an invitation to the party by answering the Dune Sea Duster Question.

If you scored 20 points or more, congratulations! Come celebrate with us. We're finally free from the clutches of the Emperor and his evil Empire!

DUNE SEA DUSTER
QUESTION

According to C-3PO, how long does it take to be digested when one falls into the belly of the all-powerful Sarlacc?
a. 100 years   b. 10 years   c. 1,000 years   d. 3,000 years

DUNE SEA DUSTER
QUESTION ANSWER

c. 1,000 years

That doesn't sound like too much fun, does it?

Were you correct? If so, get out your dancing shoes and go join the Ewoks and the heroes of the Rebellion in celebration.

If you were incorrect and scored 19 points or less, you might want to consider getting more training. You have much yet to learn, young one. Study hard and one day you may yet be of assistance to the New Republic. Keep trying!

You can come to the party anyway. It is a time of great celebration and joy!

LEVEL ONE

I. CHARACTER KNOWLEDGE

1. c
2. Jedi
3. d
4. b
5. c

II. MISSION KNOWLEDGE

6. False. He doesn't think they're powerful enough.
7. a
8. True
9. False. He's surrounded by battle droids.
10. False. They remain in the cruiser and Anakin pilots them to safety.

ANSWER KEY

LEVEL TWO

I. CHARACTER
KNOWLEDGE

1. General Grievous
2. Anakin Skywalker
3. Obi-Wan Kenobi
4. Count Dooku
5. Chancellor Palpatine
6. b
7. True
8. d
9. c
10. Padmé Amidala
11. b
12. True
13. True
14. Mace Windu
15. Padmé Amidala
16. Bail Organa
17. Yoda
18. Captain Typho
19. Mon Mothma
20. Ki-Adi-Mundi

II. DROIDS AND
VEHICLES

21. c
22. True
23. b
24. a
25. c
26. b
27. False. Anakin thinks battle droids are easy targets.
28. Battle droid
29. Droideka
30. Super battle droid
31. Vulture droid

32. Jedi starfighter
33. Federation cruiser
34. Coruscant fire ship
35. Droid tri-fighter

III. ALIENS AND
PLANETS

36. b
37. a
38. c
39. d
40. Alderaan

IV. GALACTIC
POLITICS

41. True
42. c
43. False. He doesn't really care.
44. False. Mace Windu thinks the Clone Wars should end.
45. True
46. True
47. d
48. True
49. b
50. True

LEVEL THREE

I. CONFEDERACY OF INDEPENDENT SYSTEMS KNOWLEDGE

1. c
2. b
3. d
4. a
5. b
6. False. Nute Gunray is very worried.
7. d
8. False. General Grievous is sure he will defeat Obi-Wan.
9. c
10. b

II. CHARACTER IDENTIFICATION

11. Nute Gunray
12. Shu Mai
13. Passel Argente
14. Poggle the Lesser
15. San Hill

III. WEAPONS IDENTIFICATION

16. Electrostaff
17. Wookiee blaster
18. Alderaan blaster
19. Utapau blaster rifle
20. Battle droid blaster
21. Count Dooku's lightsaber
22. c   23. a
24. d   25. b

IV. DROIDS AND VEHICLES

26. Spider droid
27. Forklift droid
28. C-3PO
29. Worker droid
30. Utapau crab droid
31. c
32. b
33. True
34. d
35. False. They require a hyperdrive ring.

V. ALIENS AND CREATURES

36. Rodian
37. Nos monster
38. Can-cell
39. Wookiee
40. Eopie

VI. GALACTIC HAPPENINGS

41. True
42. False. Yoda does not want the Chancellor to have direct control of the Jedi Council.
43. False. Anakin is upset because he has not been appointed a Jedi Master.
44. a
45. False. They accept him only hesitantly.
46. b
47. True
48. c
49. True
50. True
51. a
52. c
53. c
54. b
55. True
56. False. Yoda wants to rinse off.
57. b
58. False. Obi-Wan escapes.
59. b
60. d

ANSWER KEY

LEVEL FOUR

I. SITH KNOWLEDGE

1. True
2. c
3. b
4. True
5. a
6. a
7. d
8. c
9. True
10. a
11. c
12. b
13. False. Obi-Wan thinks he has defeated Darth Vader.
14. d

II. JEDI KNOWLEDGE

15. Agen Kolar
16. Saesee Tiin
17. Plo Koon
18. d
19. a

III. PLANETS

20. a
21. c
22. b
23. False. Obi-Wan goes to Tatooine.
24. c

IV. GALACTIC HAPPENINGS

25. True
26. False. He uses Force lightning.
27. b
28. False. Anakin does help.
29. False. Adi Gallia was on a clone BARC speeder bike.
30. b
31. c
32. a
33. b
34. True
35. b
36. True
37. False. Chancellor Palpatine takes complete control of the Senate.
38. b
39. False. Obi-Wan says he cannot fight Anakin.
40. False. Padmé believes it's best to think things through.
41. a
42. False. Chancellor Palpatine declares himself Emperor for life.
43. True
44. True
45. b
46. c
47. True
48. b
49. c
50. False. Anakin doesn't know about them.

BONUS LEVEL

I. CHARACTER KNOWLEDGE

1. b
2. c
3. c
4. Lando Calrissian
5. Admiral Ackbar
6. Grand Moff Tarkin
7. Boba Fett

II. PLANETS

8. Tatooine
9. b
10. c
11. d
12. a
13. a
14. b
15. False. Tatooine is a desert planet.

III. ALIENS AND CREATURES

16. b
17. d
18. b
19. a
20. Gamorrean guard
21. Rancor
22. Jawa
23. Ewok
24. Ugnaught

IV. DROIDS

25. False. R2-D2 is carrying the plans.
26. False. Uncle Owen purchases R5-D4 first, but R5 has a bad motivator and is returned.
27. True
28. True
29. b
30. True